CHERRY COLA

MARA NKERE

THE **BLACK SPRING**
PRESS GROUP

First published in 2021
by Eyewear Publishing Ltd / Black Spring Press Group
Grantully Road, Maida Vale, London W9,
United Kingdom

Typeset with graphic design by Edwin Smet
Author photograph Mara Nkere
Cover photograph James Haisman

ISBN 978-1-913606-83-1

*We wish to acknowledge and gratefully thank the Arts Council of England
for their funding support for this book title.*

BLACKSPRINGPRESSGROUP.COM

To all girls and boys who love Love

CHAPTER 1: **GIRL**

CHAPTER 2: **BOY**

CHAPTER 1
GIRL

CHERRY COLA

I saw this boy
and thought
of cherry cola.
Cherries marinated
in essence,
cinnamon,
nutmeg and anise,
submerged in sucrose.
I watched his mouth pucker
as he ate his lunch.

I watched his
head flutter
like a rhythmic note.

His hair,
scorching tequila, sizzling sangria.
It sparkled like flames
hitting a hydroxyl,
setting alight his head and
everything in his path:
his arched brows,
his cheekbones,
his sharp jaw.

It was a thing of beauty,
this sweet
cherry liqueur.

I blinked,
I breathed,
and then
I realised.

I knew.

IGNITE

I feel,
    I feel so light.
        I'm completely lost in these smoke loops.
            I stare at these loops, their shapes,
                their curves, their waves.
                    I feel the melodic rhythm of my heartbeat;
                    it mirrors this boy's heartbeat.
                        Our heartbeats synchronise, intertwine
                    and time rapidly bends.
                    Both beats alchemise; passion ignites,
                a passion not defined by the present
              but by a paradigm we have created.
        I look at you.
      Coyly, you smile at me.
You feel it too.

HIM

I couldn't possibly have another one, my eyes twinkled as I stared at him. This boy was breath-takingly beautiful. A shaft of sunlight streamed through the window illuminating his eyes. His gorgeous eyes. Such a mesmerising light ocean blue; rivers of pulsing life saturated his eyes with gold. They radiated with intensity and integrity. His brows were framed by strawberry blonde hair; his prominent jawline curved gracefully around his face and his nose was well defined. I moved towards him, captivated. A current of cold electricity passed through the air. The mole below his right eye twitched as he shivered. I looked at him. His playful smile had drawn into a pouty line across his face. Such perfect lips. His mesmeric beauty was heart-swelling. I reached out to touch. Then I stopped.

YOUR EXTRAORDINARY MIND

Not everyone has this boy's mind. Your mind. What's in a mind? What separates an ordinary mind from an *extra*ordinary mind? I'll tell you. Neurons rapidly signal between your left and right hemispheres, perfect balance held. Your ability to use the right brain's creativity and left brain's logic simultaneously reveals an extraordinary mind. Your extraordinary mind. These neurons accelerate into hyperspeed – 120 metres per second. Each thought catapults into different dimensions, different realms, where you're able to decipher fallacies in matters of life and death, and formulate innovative concepts.

This strand of genius, Binet's IQ test can't measure, can't behold. Rare individuals have stood out for their meteoric contributions: Einstein for his influence on the philosophy of science; Curie for her role in radioactivity, to name a few. And now you. Now you stand among them, for your extraordinary mind. For your potential to advance humanity. So that's why I keep smiling. This boy I see in front of me is one I'm exceptionally proud of. This boy I see planning his future is one I thoroughly admire. This boy I see upholding his strong moral compass is one I look to... So that's why I keep smiling.

MY BLOOD MOON

In melted darkness, I see
a blood diamond. Walls fade with the
moonlight, red splendour radiates, shadows
caress, drape over this dazed moon, a moon in
sync with the earth's disc, perfect alignment and
accord. Every tick of the clock, my insides quiver.
Soon this eclipse will be over and all I'll have are faded
memories. I wait and I wait, but the moon fades not yet
to grey. Clouds try to distort, drown the moon's face
but the moon lets out a ruby flicker. The rain tries to
quench the moon's light but the moon continues
to glow. You have eclipsed me like this moon;
like a fiery love you shine, like the moon
stabilises the earth's axis, like a pendulum
regulates a clock's speed, so has
this boy eclipsed me.

VITAMIN D

I'm deficient in vitamin D, doctor.

That musk dose is truly irresistible
on bare skin.
This woody note always starts warm;
you would pant in this sticky, tropic air.
Observe its rhythmic rise —
then the hit would change,
become harder, almost animalistic.
It would thrust its gold,
a myriad of yellows
that gleam and sparkle
until that vitamin D finally explodes and
gets completely inside of me.

COCKTAIL

I move my bourbon lips towards this boy.
I suck on his hardened crystal
and start to work on it.
I submerge it in this bourbon,
spit on it, gargle on it, choke on it,
until it dissolves into a sucrose syrup.
I add three dashes of Angostura bitters
to balance this sweetness,
garnish with mandarin peels to excite his palate,
add ice to impede the melting process.
It calms my spicy caramel notes.
His sweetness becomes pronounced;
my temperature drops rapidly
but I continue to stir.

BREAKING BREAD

Pin the dough down
Use your tongue to knead the dough
Circle the dough in one direction with your tongue –
no, just use the tip *mi amor*
Change position
Fold your tongue back on itself
Circle the dough again by 90 degrees
This time use your fingers –
work slowly
Next, turn it around
Stroke the dough firmly to knock out its air
Pull the two ends
Stretch the dough out, make it elastic
Thrust the dough with a spoon
(the fatter, the better)
Roll it up and down again rapidly
Repeat several times until smooth
You can hear the dough bubbling, can't you?

It's time

Bake me
And then *mi amor*
Fucking break me

TRANSFIXED

The air above us tingles with electric energy, stronger than anything I've felt before. My chest tightens. I want you so much. As you pull my body towards yours, my nipples become erect. The kiss hardens, my body reacts. This force overwhelms every cell, pulses as you submerge your tongue between my thighs. A different kind of air catches in my throat – it's like breathing for the first time. I move on top of you and start riding you. Slow pace, rapidly increasing. I'm groaning as the intensity grows, getting wetter with each thrust, a swell about to burst. It scorches my body like a flame, yet chills my skin like sleet flowing in unmapped waves. I'm transfixed, igniting everything trapped inside me. In your final surge, the tsunami breaks free and energy courses through every inch of my being. I lean into you and shut my eyes.

THAT FIRST

I bet you'll love me after that first stroke
I bet you'll love me when I'm drippin' in your yolk
I bet you'll love me after you get that first tide
I bet you'll love me once your seed gets all the way inside
I bet you'll love me after that first motion
I bet you'll love me when you're swimming deep
throat in this ocean

And I bet you something else m'dear
I bet it all goes downhill from here

CHESS OPENING

We're both trying
to control the four
central squares in our
love story. You're just
more forward about
it. I start. You're not
too pleased. I move
my middle

pawn forward; it
occupies one key
centre square. Your
turn, my darling boy.
You answer back by
copying my move
and staking your
claim to the

second centre
square. I move my
knight towards the
centre, applying
pressure to your
pawn. You smile, try
to seduce me with
your touch.

You copy my move
again, placing my
pawn under attack
with your knight.
I'm anxious,
unsure of my next
move. This will be
interesting.

SOLAR STRIKE

the moon is hilarious.
the earth can't stop laughing. the moon
thinks it controls the earth's tides,
completely unaware that the earth's tidal force
can slow down the moon's rotation
and has the power to lock the moon.

the moon thinks it's bigger than the earth,
completely unaware it's less than half the size
of the earth. the moon
insults the earth's kinky hair, forgetting
the earth's atmosphere protects itself from
the sun's dangerous rays.

the moon thinks it's special because it's
surrounded by the dark. the moon
states it's white, pure and luminous due
to the sunlight it reflects,
completely unaware that beyond the naked eye
it's muddy, a colour the moon hates.

the moon is hilarious.
the earth can't stop laughing. the moon
thinks no-one is able to see its craters,
completely unaware that its massive volcanoes
constantly erupt causing these craters.
look – it's happening right now.

F***

we use our mouths and utter

you fucked up
we fucked
i'm gonna fuck him up
for fuck's sake
fuck her

but they all mean the same thing
because once you're in that state of fuck
your mind isn't functioning in this realm
of normality
as you've been transported to a
construct that your mind can't
comprehend
can't ascertain
a place where decorum bows down
to emotions so the mere thought
of translating these emotions
into an acceptable form is
laughable and inconceivable
where extremities bare all
feelings penetrate the surface
it draws you deeper
as it rotates around you
grabbing its hands around
your waist
your arms
your throat

and the only thing you can do is
to fuck the fuck

OPERATING TABLE

Every word I say is dissected.
Every word I spew
is laid out on your table,
cut open with your blade.
Letters gush out of the seams,
vowels in disarray.
My verbs lay stagnant.
You reconstruct my letters;
you stitch your words together,
you grab these words,
force me to eat them.
I refuse.
You pull my mouth apart.
I have no option
but to digest.

I swallow your words whole
everytime.

INNER WOUND

This boy's emotions have no expiry date;
they constantly drown me.
I'm so attuned with his unmet needs and
unconscious motivations,
that I forgot what mine are.
I feel so cursed with this.
He doesn't understand I need to be careful.
I have to be careful with what I pick up,
everything sticks to me –
the inner workings of his mind,
any slight nuances,
his desires,
the discrepancies in his thought patterns.
His multiple energies constantly cling to me –
I'm overwhelmed.
How do I tell this boy I have no more space,
without losing him?
Perhaps it's better to lose myself to him
than lose him altogether?

Perhaps that's completely love.

MISSISSIPPI

I look at the bathroom walls,
One Mississippi
Two Mississippi
concentrate on my breathing but
I keep finding my hands on my belly.
My nails lightly trace its left side,
trace the first letter *M*
follow to *I*
swiftly move on to *S*
Three Mississippi
join to the second *S*.
I gently guide the second *I* to my belly button
but I immediately stop in my tracks.
This tracing isn't right, it looks like a heartbeat.
I'm petrified, I shout,
I'm screaming.
I can't *unsee* what I see.
Four Mississippi
My eyes look down to the blood clots,
inspect the large angry ones
between my thighs.
I realise I have no choice but to wait,
I wait to say goodbye.

PIT

The Lord led me,
I followed.
I saw the devil on her gravestone;
the devil ripped her skin open into two,
gored at her flesh, her tendons, her muscles,
broke down her bones.
I looked at the Lord,
           the Lord just watched.

THE WAKE

The girl simply wept.

'TIL FAITH DOES US APART

To this boy, my idiosyncrasy is my faith.
He's not able to see how it ebbs in fast folds,
the way it whispers to me like a lover,
places soft kisses on my cheek,
how it rouses me to wakefulness,
how it clings to my throat,
the freshness over my skin,
how its touch massages my body,
how its sound pierces my every thought
when I close my eyes. I breathe in.
This breeze that detoxifies –
I hear its lullaby
awaking all senses.
I succumb completely.

I offer you this breeze,
you urinate all over it.
I try the lullaby, instead
you laugh, throwing the lullably at me;
its chords fall over my exposed skin.

I look at myself.
I'm stained red and broken;
a crimson scream bellows outward.

20

A metal dice, this boy placed in my palm to roll.
The faces were either too cold or too hot
to the touch.
I adjusted the dice
between my two hands.
Its sharp edges pierced my pudgy flesh.
I looked at this twenty-sided dice:
some faces were scratched,
some faces were polished chrome,
some faces were a dull matte.
You see,
I can handle playing with a common dice –
a fair six-sided dice.
I can grip a six-sided dice properly.
I can throw it in the air and wait for the dice
to land on a face.
I know regardless of the times I roll,
all outcomes
will be equally probable.
I know what the expected value will be,
I can handle that probability.

I look back at this boy's dice.
I don't think I'm going to roll.

INDEFENSIBLE

If you don't roll this dice,
what's the point of being together,
this boy uttered.

In that moment,
my heart stood still
and an emotion so alien consumed me,
filled me to the point where I couldn't breathe –
it was fear.
At that point, I knew he had my heart;
he had the ability to crush my heart into
a million pieces,
to chew it up
to chomp on it
to spit on it
and there was nothing I could do but watch.

My heart,
for years I've guarded you,
but I carelessly gave a stranger the keys,
to have his way with you.
Can you forgive me?

BLACK AND JACK

Let's try a card game, this boy huffed as he led me to the table.

I can't return or exchange these two cards in my hands. I sigh heavily, outlining the race card's perimeter as I'm deep in thought. The faith card just stares at me like a night owl. I shake my head and reluctantly face this boy. *Just get on with it,* I mutter impatiently.

This boy gives me a devilish smile and highlights the five rules:

1. *You can't go over 21 points and if you do so, you lose me*
2. *Each card you're holding has a 10 point value*
3. *You can't refuse another card*
4. *You have to take another card*
5. *The next card you get will potentially range from 1–10 points*

My whole body shakes vehemently. I'm infuriated — this boy has set me up to fail. I have a 90% chance of losing him.

THE ULTIMATUM

Now I stand before you
with my heart in my hands.
I'm down on my knees boy,
accept my offering.
I need your love,
don't make me choose
between you and Christ.
Don't you know my entire
identity is fashioned
around Him?
I serve Christ.
I live for Christ.
He was pierced for my rebellion,
He was crushed for my sins,
He was beaten so I could
be healed.
Please don't make me choose boy,
because it'll always be Jesus.

LEFT AGAIN

I've been left again and disregarded.
Am I the only one with a heart in this world,
the kind of heart that feels when someone's hurt,
that comforts, that understands?
Why am I going through this cycle again,
a cycle, that calls me by name, taunts and punches me
until I'm black and blue?
I'm burnt out,
no more energy left to fight.
I'm done.
I can finally say I'm done.

CONTRACT BREACH

Is rejection avoidable? If one party rejects another party, who is to blame? The rejected or the Rejecter? Let's start again, how much self-reflection does one have to go through to feel whole again after being rejected? Who has the answers to these bloody questions? C'mon everyone, I dare you to answer at least one question.

Yes, you've guessed it, the rejected is irate. Anger doesn't quite cover this feeling. Enraged, confused and infuriated to the limit. The rejected doesn't say anything or act out when the Rejecter is suffocating the rejected with multiple messages. The rejected understands, listens and cries with the Rejecter but the minute the rejected starts needing the Rejecter that little bit more, the Rejecter shuts the rejected out.

Completely shuts the rejected out, pretends the rejected doesn't exist and that they have no impact or relevance to the Rejecter's life. Just like that. Reducing the rejected to nothing. So again, back to the question, who is to blame? The rejected or the Rejecter? One means, the rejected should have known and understood the dynamics of the relationship prior, right? Right?

Was this contract breached – did the rejected overstep the limits and boundaries in this contract? Were clinginess and neurotic behaviours only meant for the Rejecter, not the rejected?

Answer these questions! Was the rejected at fault? Should the rejected have read the contract thoroughly? The rejected should have known this relationship was on a fixed-term basis.

The rejected was never permanent.

The rejected should have known the relationship was only subject to the Rejecter's terms and conditions until the Rejecter terminated the contract. Without the need of notice.

Was the rejected at fault? Didn't the rejected read all the terms and conditions? Where it clearly states, the rejected agrees to devote their whole working time and attention to the Rejecter. Doesn't it state the rejected's performance and conduct will be monitored and the Rejecter reserves the right to make any changes in this period?

So, we're all in agreement then, it must be my fault.

PLASTICITY

1. i'm going mad. there, i've said it. isn't saying these fatal words supposed to alleviate some stress? some strain? alas, no, my heart is still gripped in this wretched vice. someone, please someone, loosen the jaws in this vice as my heart is about to plastically deform. my heart's nearing the elastic limit; the number of dislocations keeps accumulating. these dislocations continuously interact, inducing strain fields that annihilate, quickening this deformation process. these dislocations have taken hold of my surface irregularities, defects in my heart that were never fixed, never mended. these dislocations propagate; my slip planes compress; my bonds sequentially break, crack and rupture. i beg, please stop! loosen the jaws in this vice!
2. yes, i heard that,
3. i heard it snap too.

THOUGHTS

i keep thinking how much heartbreak hurts,
the severity of it,
and why no-one warned me about it.
i keep thinking of the way this boy used to hold me around my waist
while i was washing the dishes:
the way this boy's mouth would pucker before he ate food
the way his eyes would widen when he was winding me up
the way we instantaneously felt the connection in the first few hours
the way we would discuss our future together
the way i gave this boy my heart and asked him to cherish it
the way this boy knew automatically what was wrong with me
the way i was able to feel his every emotion
the way we revealed we loved each other
the way i loved this boy's scent
the way i love this boy,
and now i have, as the rule of heartbreak goes,
i have to get over this boy.
i've tried,
but i can't.
they say time heals all wounds,
but can it physically put broken pieces back together
without any remnants of scars?
my thoughts keep drifting,
keep drifting back to this boy.

A LEAK IN THE BOTTLE

This girl's hurting.
She gave all she had to this boy
and she hasn't gotten anything back.
The love he had for her
slowly leaks out of his being,
daily.
She can feel it leaving.
She tries to collect it,
tries to hold onto it,
tries to store his cherry cola,
but it keeps dripping from her hands.

WEB TENSION CONTROL

i'm tackling the most uncomfortable subject
which is myself,
a girl lost in the labyrinths of her own web.
everywhere i run, there's something blocking my escape,
that sweet short-lived escape.
tension keeps building in my web.
my regulator is broken:
a girl unable to create the optimal tension set-point
a girl unable to generate the signal for her internal dancer roller
a girl unable to lower this roller to reduce her brake pressure
a girl unable to repair her shaft encoder
so this roller refuses to move –
it's stuck.
pull too tight, you'll distort my web;
don't pull tight enough, you'll break my web.

shush,
just skip the small talk.
wind me until this tension is released.
increase the speed of your motor, boy.
i said skip the small talk.
i don't want your love or your heart, boy –
just unwind my web.

LIKE CLOCKWORK

this boy still comes to me
three days a week
two hours a session
without fail

he sits in that same chair
inserts two thin needles in his arm
connects the needles to a tube
attaches the tube into me

before i know
his blood passes into me
i filter his waste, solutes and toxins
and pass back the purified blood

after the session
he removes the needles and tube
applies a plaster on his arm
and just walks out

every fucking time

QUICK RECIPE

First, cut off his dick
Take that frozen stick
Grate and grind it
Expose this stick to sharp edges –
cut through it
Add this to flour
Pulse the mixture –
really use your fingertips
to knead that flour
Pre-heat the oven to 180C
Liquefy his brain in a blender
Combine this runny mixture
with his heart shards in a small
saucepan over a low heat
Cook and stir for five minutes
until all pieces are deformed
Transfer this bloody blend
into an ovenproof dish
Sprinkle the flour mixture
on top
Bake in the oven –
forty minutes until burnt
and the bloody blend
is bubbling
Serve with thick cream

What?
What are you looking at, my darling?
Dig in!

THE 'C' WORD

you call me crazy
you don't know crazy
if crazy isn't pouring cyanide
on your open cuts
if its calloused claw isn't gripping
your collar
if steel shavings aren't squeezing
your spine
if crazy isn't skinning you like a cheetah
ripping your carcass open
freeing your intestines

so call me crazy again
and
see what will happen

LOST

I walk close to this mirror
and observe —
a face with no eyes
a sallow complexion
a face etched with lines
etched with immense sadness
a face full of crippling pain.
Who is this girl?
Is this what I have become?
I don't know who this girl is.
Slowly I move my face to bed
and just lie down willing myself to sleep.
Sleep doesn't come.
Memories of this boy have turned into
vicious nightmares;
thoughts of lost potential and broken promises gore my
being
giving rise to acute levels of pain and inflammation.
With every minute
my chest becomes heavy,
my palpitations increase.
This sound is tormenting me;
the stressed low notes are too exaggerated against the
silence,
this chord is too pronounced,
this beat is too pronounced.
I cannot sleep.
I just want to sleep.
I feel uneasy.
I cannot cope with this ordeal.
I'm not even sure what part of me is dying
or if I'm already dead.

THE CANDLE

The candle just sat in the corner,
distant.
Her gaze shifted over to the crackling cracks on
the ceiling.
Cobwebs came out to play;
strands of dirty lace
fought the banister while the black mould
stared at the candle.
The black mould began to laugh as it
clasped itself around her wax,
choking her.
It pinned down the candle
forcing her wick to the flame.
The candle screamed,
desperate to avoid the fire,
pleading with the black mould.
The flame hissed and slithered to her wick –
the once white, pure wick was now
charred and blackened.
The fire travelled rapidly downwards
to her body,
melting the wax nearest to her wick.
The candle's melted wax vaporised,
her internal molecules were broken down
and were drawn into the fire.

Sadly, the torture continued.
This heat was drawn down again
to melt more of her wax.
Hot vapours were squeezed from her wick
as oxygen from the air fuelled the flame.
The hungry flame started to sneer and ebb,

it continued to feed on her wax,
devouring her hollow core.
The candle began to weep silently
as her molten tears and unburned carbon
dripped down her thin walls.
She closed her eyes and accepted her fate.

In the abyss
a breeze floated into the room
like a pulsating butterfly.
It placed soft kisses on her walls
and wiped her molten tears.
The breeze caressed the candle,
solidifying her distressed wax.
It blew a thin stream of air,
quenching the fire.
From her wick, a wisp of silver smoke
waltzed upwards
as it entwined with the breeze.
The breeze and her smoke danced wildly.
They danced like the nightingale who sings,
spiralling into the sweetest of swirls –
tantalising twists in every twirl
until both whirled together
into the wind.

LADY IN RED

With red lipstick
I no longer feel like a girl.
It's that exposure I fear,
so I paint over that
sultry fear:
start with the cupid bow,
then with the edge,
and finish with the centre
of the lip.
You know God doesn't like ugly,
so everyday
I perfect this:
break into my medicine cabinet,
pop those little red pills,
apply, wipe off, reapply.
My little red pills.
I get messy sometimes.
Can't help but gravitate towards
the darker reds,
the erotic merlots.
I stare at my lips intensely,
slightly parted like labia —
bloodstained, wrinkled folds.
Thick crimson beads bleed
into my skin,
crawl into my mouth —
damn,
this blood tastes so sweet.

CHAPTER 2
BOY

CHERRY COLA

Another day, just like every other.
It was getting close to lunch and my stomach
was rumbling.
Little did I realise, my heart would soon
be fumbling.
Walking into the hustle and bustle,
as I queued for food, I almost pulled a muscle.
I strained my neck to look at the end
of the table.
In attempting to believe it, I was
certainly unable.
For sat in the corner was a pelicular sight,
and my cheeks had risen to 100 degrees Fahrenheit.
Perhaps she was temporary, a flying visitor?
But with so many questions I had become the
inquisitor.
Low and behold, an incredible thing,
as into my step was a newfound spring,
for just around the corner, who would I find?
It was the very girl still so fresh on my mind.
Cherry Cola, she called me.
Her smile boomed like a boisterous sea.
With an extended hand and a glint in her eyes
I was immediately hooked, to my surprise.
As I hung to every word so eloquently spoken,
I knew this girl would already leave me broken.
For this was only the beginning of a whole
new chapter –
and my heart? She was its captor.

51

THIS GIRL

You linger like a drug in my bloodstream
refusing to metabolise –
your mind is my ecstasy
your touch is my heroin
your breath is my meth
your words are narcotic
rendering me helpless.
My mind is on speed
whenever I see you.
I'm hooked on you –
I need a fix.
I can take it
just a
hit.
I   promise –
just
one   more
hit.

HER

This girl cannot see her beauty.
She cannot see her caramelised complexion,
the way it glazes smoothly over her bones.
She cannot see the rings of onyx fire in her eyes.
The warmth of her onyx deepens
as her fluttery lashes dance on the peripheral
with increasing intensity –
each flutter reacts with the onyx
turning her flame into ash.
Her eyes, now smoky coal:
marked, memorable, distinct.
Her gaze has me paralysed;
it crawled under my tendons,
stamped its territory in my brain.
Her gaze makes my blood sing.

This girl cannot see her beauty
but hopefully, this girl can see the spell
she has put on me.

BURNT SIENNA

There's beauty in death,
a certain seduction in burning sienna.
I gaze at her nakedness,
watch her mahogany glisten.
I kneel towards this girl's smoky quartz
and trace the down-curve of her full lips.
My lips brush on hers,
she presses her tongue against mine;
I surrender completely.
Her glow is hypnotising;
this fiery burn penetrates all layers,
the heat weaves into my skin,
dissolves my flesh
limb by limb.
Her breath quickens; my pain intensifies –
but I can't let go.

CRAVINGS

I crave this girl,
that intimacy
that attracts the ear
that bubbles the brain
that pricks the flesh
that raises the flesh
that makes my heart skip a beat
that intimacy
with no filters
no boundaries
no borders —
I crave this girl.

JUNGLE FEVER

I've always fucked black girls.
Big butts, bodacious curves, chocolate skin –
chocolate skin makes me shake, shiver,
salivate uncontrollably.

There are two options really –
I could either drink
or eat this chocolate.

Option 1
Melt this chocolate until it gleams,
pour that silky texture down my throat,
taste those spicy aldehydes.
Just thinking about it makes me hard.

Option 2
Inhale that cacao, I ache for it,
watch the way it snaps when I break it.
I could just bite into it, piece by piece,
let the chocolate dissolve on my tongue.

This girl's my Jezebel.
I fantasise about that next contact,
Cherry Cola on Coca-Cola.

COMPOTE

Her pussy tastes like fig compote.
I wipe her thick dark skin with my tongue,
paint deep circles at the peak,
squeeze this peak with my fingers —
it splits.
I see fuchsia...
Milky sap erupts from the seams
and drizzles out of the base,
the sap crystallises on the surface.

A blend of bourbon emanates.
I bathe in this ditzy daze of liqueur.
Quickly the firm crunch of
white musk and sandalwood dominates.
My notes temper this concoction,
add a sharpness that soothes
her crystal lines.
The greater the hit, the moister her interior —
I dive in completely and feast.

REACTION TYPE QUIZ

Split her atom and you get what?
hint

use a neutron to penetrate her atom
watch the neutron hide in her atom's pulsing

slippery walls

watch the neutron begin   to thrust
watch the neutron thrust   faster and   deeper
watch how her atom   crackles,   snaps

watch her juicy atom gargle on that neutron

and moans at increasing pressure

until it vibrates and completely destabilises

watch the neutron   explode

as the rush
intensifies

watch as the neutron flips her atom around

her atom open

gently spreading

out

watch how the neutron rolls
up and down her
inclined plane
the way it paints intricate circles inside
her atom
watch how her atom leaks
with every stroke
watch how the neutron bends
her atom over
grabs her proton from its nucleus
grabs both faces
it
rims her proton
devours her proton

stretches

hint over
Can you guess my type of reaction, my love?

I'M HIGH

I'm inside a cloud, in an air balloon drifting away. The wheels in my head have stopped... Can't I always feel like that? I'm numb but I'm lost in this girl's mind, lines and skin. I embrace the cage of our beat. The pitch stretches and slowly bends the time. The beat doesn't stop; it rapidly increases with every stroke and sends me down a secret path within myself. Suddenly the space around us shifts, expands into a new dimension, and the rhythm changes again becoming sweet.

I have completely become one with you.

I sink into this extreme pleasure with no agenda.

Just me and this girl – we're indefinable.

Just me and this girl – the heat within us rises.

Just my skin on my girl's skin.

INSATIABLE

Three things I know to be true –
my insatiable curiosity to learn
my insatiable hunger to read
and my insatiable love for you
my sweet Cola.

LOVE LESSON

Good evening class, gather your notepads. I have something special to discuss.
Love, there I've said it. Albeit without the fatal *I* and *You* attached to either side.
Now class, settle down, this is an important lesson – how does one define love?
Yes, you at the back.

Is love eternal and unconditional?
Does love derive from intimacy and sexual connection?
Is love giving the person keys to your heart?
Is love a deep affection and nothing more?
Is… Is…

Class, settle down, too many questions at once!

Define love, teacher!

Do you really want to know?

Love is messy and subjective, my students. It is the purest form of humanity; it resides within each of us and is only defined by us. It's more than that electric spark you get when you kiss someone, touch them and interact with them.

Love is when you have a reason to come back home, a reason to justify your existence. You know you're in love when you can't imagine living without this person and you'll do anything to have this person by your side.

You cannot see love students, you cannot taste love, but you can feel this bond when you're around this person.

Love, my students, is what makes you want to wake up tomorrow. Because without it you're a mere corpse.

Class dismissed.

AROMATHERAPY

I bet you smell as good as you taste, I said.

This girl looked at me and laughed,
moved my head to the base of her throat.
Smell me again, she whispered.
Her top note was fresh and light,
a headfuck of citrus curls,
mandarin mist of flirty freshness
artificially breezy,
but it evaporated quickly
once she had me.

Her actual heart note burst in.
I was forced to smell her properly;
the olfactory clashes of tuberose,
smell her camphorous facets.
It was too carnal this tuberose,
I couldn't restrain or manage this.

You moved my head lower,
this time to your cleavage.
The smell intensified,
your complexity deepened.
The tuberose mingled and intertwined
with tonka bean.
Tonka is utterly moody, dark and spicy,
it doesn't like to be bothered.
In its dry down, this base note caramelised to
toxic, peppery coumarin.

You should've warned me
but it's my fault,
I wanted to swim in your scent, after all.

MOOD SWINGS

17th Feburary 10:54
Her hips push back, knees slightly bend, feet turn
slightly out and her shoulders pull back. She's set.
This girl's mood swings backwards.

17th Feburary 14:16
She snaps her hips forwards, keeps her shins vertical and
her heels rooted solidly to the ground.
This girl's mood swings forwards.

17th Feburary 15:27
This girl's mood is at shoulder height.

17th Feburary 16:30
As her mood swings down, her abs brace. She brings her
mood close to her chest.

17th Feburary 18:04
She crouches down to a low position.

17th Feburary 18:32
She moves back into neutral.

17th Feburary 19:17
She moves her mood two inches from her body.

17th Feburary 20:02
Her hips push back, ribs pull down and her mid-back
expands as she inhales.
This girl's mood swings backwards.

17th Feburary 22:12

She pushes her hips forwards and keeps her neck in neutral. This girl's mood swings forwards.

She repeats this mood cycle for 15 reps, takes a 30-second break and then repeats for 100 sets.

PICK

Girls like to pick at things
Girls pick at their situations, pick at their food
Girls pick at each other's brains, and then pick some more
Girls pick at their clothes, pick at their flaws
Pick at beneath, pick with their claws
Pick and prod and punch and poke
Until nothing remains, their fingertips sore
Picking and picking and picking away

ENDOTHERMIC

I can't
get inside —
The biting cold has stung her skin into clumsy numbness,
the cold stalks her like a shark,
the bitter wind snarls as the cold gradually seeps into her heart
and spreads painfully throughout her nerves.
This girl is so cold now, she pricks
with every touch I make.
She steals my heat,
she chills my blood and gnaws at my insides.
With every kiss,
there are always intermediates —
our chemical bonds don't quite form,
our chemical bonds don't quite break.
We're just in this uncomfortable transition state.
I'm trying to initiate an actual reaction
but she keeps absorbing my energy.
I'm gradually losing her —
I can't
keep doing this.

MONA LISA

Colour is false advertising.
You don't believe me?
Take the Mona Lisa:
leave it in the heat,
watch the colours seep out
like scattered sheep,
see the colours try to
withstand the light,
but they can't –
they can't coalesce.
Instead the pigments manipulate
each other,
destroy the saturation within
themselves.

Until what's left
is an ugly damaged Lisa.

LOSS

When the loss is so bitter,
you cough and choke on it
until you're swimming
in phlegm.
You try to spit it out –
you can't.
Your arteries constantly dilate
and contract;
you're gasping for air
begging for my help.

I need you to remember baby,
you went ahead and
swallowed the pill.
I was the last one to know –
you pulled the trigger first.

LOGIC

If I don't think about
what this girl did
then it didn't happen.

COTTON CANDY

I have an urge to touch every black baby's hair:
the dark clouds of molten sugar,
the tangled mess of inky swirly lollies,
the avalanche of liquorice curls –
honestly, *you people* and your hair.

LOVE GAME

I slipped on the grass and injured my knee,
now I'm going to SUE this tournament.
Who changed the surface without my consent?
I'm so livid.

Playing on clay was easy.
I dominated on clay.

My heavy topspin kicked off the clay,
this girl couldn't return my shots.

My balls bounced higher,
friction slowed her balls.

I played her balls at my own pace.
I had time to think about my next shot,
I could even get to her drop-shots.
I wore her down with my rallies —

this girl practically moved
from side
to side.

I don't know how to play on this grass.
    The ball is coming to me at a different angle.
It bounces lower; it skids off the surface,
it's tougher to return.
            The grass is worn out,
    I cannot even return a single one.
awkward bounces are becoming ubiquitous.
I can't predict her shots,
    I can't properly adapt to her serve,
            I can't balance on this court.
My posture is weakening by soaked apparel,
icy rain keeps pouring.
Its blackened wetness coats my eyes,
I can't see her,
    I can't see her balls.
            my view is obscured –
        I don't know what her next shot will be.
    I just want to forfeit this match.

EVIDENCE

I'm not coping fine, girl.
Show me evidence for your god.
I just believe in one less god than you.
You dismiss the other gods,
so understand why I dismiss your own god:
god isn't real,
god is a lie,
god doesn't exist.
Are you really that dense?
Show me evidence for your god.

You say your bible?
A 2,000 year old archaic book riddled in
inconsistencies,
from the creation fable
to the glaring contradictions in
the law of Moses?

Why is it alright for you to wear jewellery
and eat pork?
Doesn't your precious book forbid it?
Doesn't your precious book justify the
enslavement of people?
Doesn't your precious book approve of
human sacrifice?

Stop shaking your head.
Read your bible.

SYNTAX ERROR

We're just not working.
The formula in this calculator doesn't make sense.
We keep getting *syntax ERROR*.
We keep pressing the <left> or <right> keys
to try to fix this formula
but nothing seems to work:
we've changed the angle mode from degree to radian
we've put excess brackets in this formula
we've substituted the [(-)] function for the [-] function
we've removed unnecessary letter expressions
we've deleted unwanted memory data
we've re-set this calculator multiple times.

Honestly,
the most logical thing is
to cancel this formula and press [AC].

ASSAULT

Religion raped my girl –
crept up like a thief in the night.
I heard him panting,
the pleasure in his breath,
his hands grasped around my girl's neck
marking his territory.
As his breath intensified, so did his grip.
My girl's eyes rolled back;
his stubby fingers slid down,
unbuckled her jeans –
the pounding was instant.
I can't stop shaking.
I'm so angry –
when I see this Religion,
I'm going to kill this beast.

SKY DADDY

And whilst we're being honest?
Yes, you are to some extent mentally ill.

This girl has conversations with a god who isn't real,
this girl thinks an invisible sky daddy is talking to her —
working his power through her
in some unknown mystical language.

Love is patient, Love is kind, it is not rude.

I told this girl, *Don't curse me with that quote.*
You think that a god loves and cares for you,
protects you always,
but there are people all over the world dying —
what makes you so special?

To me, believing this is a sure sign of insanity.
To me, believing this is what makes you crazy.

THE TEST

Give me the gun —
come on, it's my turn to pull the trigger.
You know we both can't survive this toxicity.

I don't know who's more mentally ill:
the girl who hears voices and believes in god,
shuts down completely,
picks at me for everything;
or the boy paralysed in negativity,
in deep depression,
his volcanos constantly haemorrhaging.
It's almost comical.
It's my turn to pull the trigger.
17% probability isn't bad.
I need to end this toxicity.
I need to pick —
Me or *You*.

Come on, boy.
Pull the trigger, don't hesistate —
just fucking shoot.

MY MAJOR

I specialise in **Regret.**

One look at me, as you drink in the curl of my lip, the set grimace, the deep pucker between my brows, you'd think anger, right? Sadness, maybe, but you're not too far off. No, what you're looking for is **regret**; that vacant look in my eyes is a good pointer, the infinitesimal shake of my head brings you warmer. That's me ruminating endlessly over my failures and mistakes, round and round and round, and round the track, I run; I run not for glory, but to shake off the cramps somehow, the cobwebs that cloud my mind, to make sense somehow of what I've done, what I'm left in.

It doesn't help, it never helps, and yet I still run, and run and run, over the same pebbles, the same lines, the same tracks hoping that maybe just this once, the track will change, but it's still a circle, a closed loop, a futile exercise, fruitless exertion. I feel **regret** on the tip of my tongue, feel it cascading over me in waves, unfurling from my core, extending to my toes and fingers, ascending to my head – *I should have been there for this girl, I shouldn't have left this girl. She* needed *me.*

Waves and waves of **regret** crash against me, hit me until I'm blue and black in my face, with questions I never want to answer but try to anyway – *Why did you do that? Why didn't you do that? Why can't you be better? Why, why, WHY!*

The saddest thing of all, I can never change the outcome. I run that track, and then once my joints ache, when they shake with exhaustion, burdened by the weight I carry,

I descend deeper into a pit of my creation reinforced by **self-hatred, pain, guilt and shame** and so begins the transition into **depression and anger** – they're all friends, these fucking emotions. **Regret** works overtime, then the others take over whenever they feel it sink; I sink into my pit and wallow, I sit there and cry, but worst of all I sit there and think even when my joints have turned to dust, my brain can't grant me this one blessing and switch itself off.

It comes with its own backup generator: 24/7, 365 days a year it powers on without fail. *Why can't you just leave me the hell alone?* I say. *Oh, so now you want to ask questions*, it spits back, *Try facing the demons of your past instead?*

With that, it opens an archive into **my greatest mistakes** with this girl. I sit there and rifle through each slide, my face turning a deeper shade of puce. Don't ever forget the saying *misery loves company*. Why should I only share the pain of one shitty memory? Open the vault, open the gates, let's drink ourselves stupid to the tune of my saddest **regrets**!

I can't ever go back and rectify my mistakes, clean up my decisions, clean up my face, wash away the pain and hurt of my choices, unsheathe the layers of ingrained **stupidity.** I need it to stop, I need it to go away, but wishing it and actually obtaining it are two separate things.

Another reminder, life is too cruel, it makes time for no-one 'cos if I could, of course, I'd go back to that day, but there isn't an *if,* there isn't a choice.

These mistakes of my past sit here with me in my pit, continue to **haunt, burden** and keep me tethered to the ground as I count them daily, running and running and running, chasing after my every wrong and infraction.

Rise up from the ashes, they say. Tell you what, I'll rise up when I can see an escape, when I can see beyond these four walls. Until then I'll bid you farewell, and hope to catch you on graduation day, when I'll be seated at the back, holding aloft my **PhD in Regret**.

TRANSLATOR WANTED

A translator is required to interpret my acidic fumes into more appropriate matter. This translator needs to have an excellent command of the two languages to ensure the translated version conveys the original meaning to this girl.

Working hours are usually 9 a.m. to 9 p.m.

- Salary will vary according to your qualification.
- Skills include having a subject knowledge specific to the content being translated.
- Excellent writing skills are necessary.

As time is of the essence, the trial period will include translating the following text to the girl:

To Girl! Stop sending me your heartbroken thoughts.
Message that abuse to somebody else.
Not Me.
You know what? I won't allow this abuse.
I won't allow you blaming me for everything.
Go to your god to help you,
I thought your god was your support system.
Has he decided to do his usual disappearing act?

THIS MEANS THIS MEANS THIS

I often feel overwhelmed.
It will sneak up on me,
a thief in the night,
as dawn yields to dusk
and before I realise it
before I even understand what's happening,
I feel the familiar ache,
the weight of my tears
escaping their ducts.
They leave trails down my face
that I trace with my fingers
down my cheek, past my jaw
back up to my nose.
A sniffle, huff, blow,
then I wipe down my tears
and turn my face back to stone.
I don't get it,
can't quite comprehend it.
A trigger they say:

Too much time thinking about this girl?
Too much time thinking about what I lost?
Too much time spent plugging holes in my head?
My heart?

I feel so alone with this,
isolated with this
but I don't know what *this* quite is.
What does *this* even mean?
I don't want to feel this.
I just want to feel whelmed
not over or under,

just the normal amount.
Goldilocks was on to something
she wanted to feel just right.

PERFECT

I still love this girl.
I miss your beautiful smile,
especially that beauty mark on the
right side of your mouth,
how it wobbles
when you laugh at me.
You were perfect in every way.

OVERDOSE

[Note: This review contains spoilers for 'Overdose']

So let's recap this week's episode, shall we?

The girl refused to give me a hit so
I screamed at her
She quietly agreed and presented herself
I completely lost grip
I consumed her
I drank her in like a starving animal
I took too much of her
I didn't mean to
The high only lasted for 2 hours
So I needed more Cola
I needed to avoid that unpleasant crash
So I had to take her at a higher dose
My brain started to bleed
I had lost the ability to repair myself
Acids began to eat away at my enamel
Causing my teeth to fall out
But I still craved her

CALENDAR INVITATION

Dear Boy,

I hope this email finds you well.

I appreciate this invitation is quite late in the day and I appreciate your understanding and flexibility.

You have been invited to be a significant part of our team.

Education and Required Experience
- Preferably a PhD / Masters in Regret from a leading institution
- Minimum A grade in self-hatred
- Inability in dealing with emotions including but not limited to pain, guilt, shame and anger
- Good exposure to recent shame
- A deep knowledge of loneliness is an advantage

Key Responsibilities Include
- Feeling despondent and hopeless
- Inability to feel joy and pleasure
- Developing a low intolerance level and feeling constantly agitated
- Doing the aforementioned without questioning me

Please note that <u>you are required</u> to accept this invitation. Further details shall be sent to you in due course once these have been finalised.

I look forward to your response.

Yours sincerely,

Your Subconscious Mind

THE 'C' WORD

I'm pretty sure I'll die of cancer
I'm not too concerned with the type
I'm just certain it'll be a cancer
I say this because
I repel everything, everyone
Something must be rotting inside me
The decay leaches out
My pungent smell scares them off
The wires in my brain constantly
try to escape
with every attempt more drastic than the first
My anger, daily, violently assaults me
tries to rip out of my body
through my mouth, my hands, my cock
It doesn't care – it just needs to break out
You see, even my fucking emotions
don't want me
They all just want out
I'm simply uninhabitable
Pretty soon, my cells will wise up and
follow suit
They will turn on me like these emotions
My cells will loathe being part of me
They will mutate, turn abnormal
They will grow and divide rapidly
become a tumour
They will squeeze, choke, block
break free from its membranes
spread throughout my bloodstream
turn all my organs against me
continue to spread

So I just wait for the cancer to get me
Finish me off
So I can finally turn off

I'M TIRED

I'm tired of feeling heavy.
A weight presses on my mind.
If only it'll vanish, and free me from its paralysing hold.
I've had to relearn the most basic of things,
breathing for instance.
A simple *inhala, exhala*, won't suffice.
I count out my breaths like sheep.
The air doesn't quite fill my lungs.
Sometimes I think it's all there, the weight's gone
but then I breathe out
and it's a choked breath, a strangled thing.
I must only have one lung.
Breathing shouldn't be this laboured?
Of course, that weight creeps back,
an extension from my mind and down into my chest,
my bones, and sadly my heart.

THIS PLACE

Being on this earth isn't doing you any good.

It really isn't, boy. The next sixty seconds will feel like an eternity.
Don't forget, there was a time when you used to care. It seems hard to
believe that you once wanted to make a difference, but I guess things
have changed.

Is it always the case that the steady, reliable passage of time will
inevitably knock it out of you? You look around and see old,
weathered, but undoubtedly wise faces. The very same faces that have
lived your potential life out several times between them. Is that what
you want? Do you want to be like them? Perhaps it is inevitable. After
all, you can't win with the losing hand.

This black cloud has been prowling closely lately. Each passing day
adding to the mockery of your position. Whatever happened to you
boy? You were ready to conquer the world with this girl, but now
every passing minute feels like an eternity.

Of course, you continue to dwell in self-pity and massage the
pretence of being wronged by this girl and the universe, to convince
yourself that cruel factors have prevented you from reaching your
true potential. That is certainly the comfortable option, passing the
buck to the seemingly hard, deterministic injustice of the universe.
But you know it isn't true. You know that this is not the fault of
any externality, and is, in fact, a result of your reluctance to claim
responsibility for your own failures.

Perhaps this is how it is for the majority of the people you surround
yourself with. At some point in time, it must have been far easier for
them to keep their position in the queue for conformity and muted
expectation.

EULOGY FOR LOVE

I want to start this Eulogy by thanking everyone for being here today.

It hasn't been easy for those who have watched our Love bloom to deal with its passing. Our Love faced a physical battle but also an emotional and mental one.

Our Love will be remembered not only as the very essence of loyalty and beauty, but as a vibrant partner. This Love was beautiful inside and out and when it glowed, I felt very much alive.

This Love was everything to me, and I miss it terribly. Love would want the girl and I to pick ourselves up, try not to give up on life and pursue a form of Love in the things that inspire us.

Love was truly good-hearted and put all things before it. This Love found time to be an amazing force to this girl and myself and for that, I am incredibly grateful.
Love was talented as it could draw this girl and myself closer together.

I'm a broken boy because this Love is gone.

This Love was born on the 27th of September and grew exponentially. It was a large ball of energy and just kept growing.
However, this Love never got the chance to advance and learn as it was too busy trying to compete with its siblings.

You see, regrettably, the girl and I spent more time catering to the others: Anger, Sorrow, Depression and our Differences, rather than Love.

This girl and I forgot to nurture this Love, feed it and develop it.
On Love's last day, it was roaming around like a bag of bones and I just didn't care.

I feel such shame now.

I was convinced that Grief and Religion murdered this Love, but ladies and gentlemen, I have to admit something. Love died because of us. Because of myself and this girl. In Love's last breath, it died because it was malnourished.

We were Love's only life. Love would do anything for us but it wasn't reciprocated. It never lost hope that the girl and I would return back to Love.

I will miss so many things about Love. I will miss its ability to make me happy. I will miss its optimism. I will miss its warmth. I will miss its light.

It's been a great privilege to write this Eulogy to express the anguish and hurt that the girl and I both share over losing Love.

I hope in due time you'll forgive us, sweet Love.

And I hope to see you very soon, my sweet Cola.

ACKNOWLEDGEMENTS

I want to express my deepest gratitude to my friend, Sapna, for giving me this idea to write a poetry book and her enthusiastic encouragement. She insisted on how relatable this topic is to all genders; this story needed to be written down and shared to all. I want to extend my thanks to my sister, Muna, and my editors, Cate and Todd, for their editing skills and valuable suggestions.

Finally, I want to thank God and my family – I am forever grateful for their unconditional love and support.